Sweet Disaster

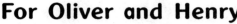

For Oliver and Henry

Find out more about **Ricky Rocket** at
www.shoo-rayner.co.uk

ORCHARD BOOKS
338 Euston Road, London NW1 3BH
Orchard Books Australia
Hachette Children's Books
Level 17/207 Kent St, Sydney, NSW 2000

ISBN 1 84616 037 5 (hardback)
ISBN 1 84616 392 7 (paperback)

First published in 2006 by Orchard Books
First paperback publication in 2007

Text and illustrations © Shoo Rayner 2006

1 3 5 7 9 10 8 6 4 2 (hardback)
1 3 5 7 9 10 8 6 4 2 (paperback)

Printed in Great Britain
Orchard Books is a division of Hachette Children's Books

Sweet Disaster

Shoo Rayner

ORCHARD BOOKS

Ricky Rocket stood in the middle of the supermarket, staring. He looked as if he'd found the Holy Grail.

"Look, Mum...Lord Vorg crunchy bars!"

LORD VORG
THEY'RE CRUNCHY
LORD VORG
CRUNCHY BARS
LORD VORG
CRUNCHY BARS
CRUNCHY BARS

"Lord Vorg's a crunchy munch!"
sang Ricky's little sister, Sue.

Ricky grabbed Sue in a martian headlock. No one made fun of Lord Vorg. He was Ricky's favourite teevee character.

Sue let out the kind of ear-splitting, blood-curdling, brain-jamming scream that little Earth girls are famous for all over the universe.

"Ricky, let her go!" Mum read the back of the packet. "These Lord Vorg bars are full of horrible chemicals! Heaven knows what they'll do to you."

"They might make me grow up to be strong and brave like Lord Vorg!"

"I don't want you growing up like HIM!" Mum said. "We'll make some proper biscuits at home."

LORD VORG FOODS

Crunchy Bars

Sugar free but full of additives. These include Xz72, Yw38 and Grdbildj. (Mmm – tasty!)

Breakfast Cereal

Power-packed with vitamins and crunchiness. There's always a fab free gift inside.

FREE! Mum-immobiliser!

Breakfast Milk

Made from crushed neetle pods. Perfect on Lord Vorg Breakfast Cereal.

Crunchy Yogurk

The meal you can take with you. In two compartments to keep the crunch fresh.

Shortbread Astronauts were Granny Earth's best recipe. Ricky and Sue mixed and rolled flour, butter and sugar, and cut out astronaut shapes.

"Mine looks like Lord Vorg!" said Ricky.

"Lord Vorg's a silly biscuit!" Sue chanted.

The kitchen filled with the wonderful smell of baking. When the oven went "Ping!", Mum took out the golden biscuits and put them aside to cool.

The doorbell rang.

A green alien stood on the doorstep with five children.

"Hello," she twinkled. "I'm Mrs Tweetle, your new neighbour."

Mum was flustered. Mrs Tweetle's husband was Dad's new boss.

"It would be an honour if you would enter our humble home and partake of some refreshment," Mum said in her posh alien voice. "A cup of tea, perhaps?"

"Tea would be lovely," Mrs Tweetle smiled. "Everyone in the universe likes Earth tea."

"Do you have milk in your tea?"
Mum asked.

"Yes please, but no sucrose,"
Mrs Tweetle's eyes bobbled. "Tweetles
are hyper-allergic to sucrose." Then
she whispered, so that Ricky couldn't
quite hear. "It makes us go a bit
silly...like being drunk!"

SHORTBREAD ASTRONAUTS

2 units flour
2 units butter
1 unit fine sugar
1 unit ground rice
(also known
as soggyleena)

Get an adult or a
Dwoolog* to help.

Mix sugar and
butter in a bowl.
Work in the flour and ground rice.
Roll out the dough
and cut to shape.
Cook in oven at 150C
until golden brown and delicious.
Allow to cool before eating.

***Dwoologs**, from the planet Dwoo,
are the best chefs
in the universe.

The Tweetles were very shy.
They stared at Ricky and Sue,
who stared back.

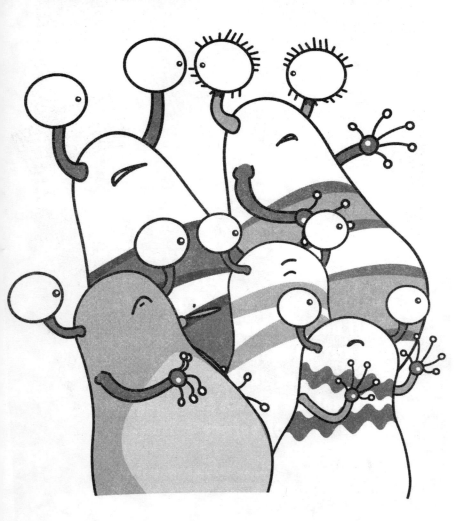

"Wanna see my rocket?" Ricky
said at last.

They followed him into the yard,
like obedient puppies.

"See my Lord Vorg laser holes?"
Ricky asked, pointing out the stickers
on the hull. "You get them free with
Vorg Flakes."

The Tweetles smiled politely.

"Fancy a ride?" Ricky asked.

The Tweetles huddled together
and shook their heads.

"Want a go on my gravity slide?" Sue climbed to the top and whizzed down the other side.

One of the
Tweetles followed
her. It sat at the
top of the slope
and didn't move.

BIG
G

Ricky was surprised. "You don't
weigh much, do you?" He turned up
the slide's gravity control.

The gravity motor whirred.
The Tweetle shot down the slide,
scooted across the yard and
crashed into a prickly bush.

The other Tweetles' eyes bobbled.
"Err, sorry," said Ricky, smirking.
"I must have turned the gravity up
to full power by mistake."

Ricky couldn't think of anything else
to do with the strange, silent creatures.

"Let's have our own tea party!"
Sue suggested, leading everyone
into the kitchen.

"Here you are," she said, pouring
water from her toy teapot into plastic
cups and saucers. "A nice cup of tea."

"Pass them round!" she ordered.
Her eyes landed on the shortbread
astronauts on the baking tray.

"Would you partake of a shortbread
astronaut?" she asked, copying Mum's
posh alien voice. "Earthlings find
them delicious."

"I like to bite their heads off first,"
said Ricky.

The Tweetles opened their mouths, threw the biscuits in, swallowed them whole and burped.

"Pardon!" they said together. It was the first word they had spoken.

TWEETLE FOOD

Tweetles have to be very careful about what they eat. They are **allergic** to many foods.

Grdbildj is an important part of the Tweetle diet. It is made from pulverised **Grd beans.**

Tweetles have **five stomachs.** They work like fermenting tanks. If sugar is added, any food in the stomach will be turned into alcohol.

Alcohol makes Tweetles so **light-headed** they are able to **float.**

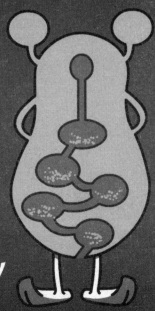

The smallest Tweetle was the first
to go funny. His eyes glazed over
and he started giggling. Soon, the
others joined him, kicking their
legs in the air.

"Laughing Landy Lizards!" Ricky
exclaimed. "They're floating!"

The five Tweetles shrieked. They
joined hands above the cooker and
swirled about like a merry-go-round.

"It's all your fault!" said Sue.
"Do something!"

"I didn't do anything!" Ricky knew
he was going to get the blame anyway.

The biggest Tweetle wafted out of
the door and into the yard.

"Come back!" Ricky yelled. It was too late. The door of his rocket was hissing shut.

The Tweetle stuck out a purple tongue and waved.

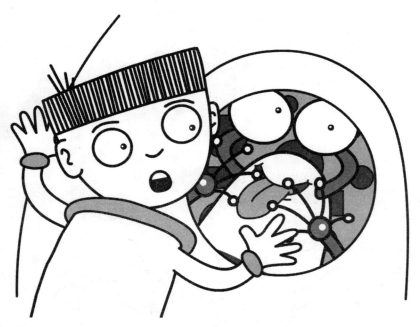

The engine throbbed. Ricky shouted and banged on the door. "You don't know how to fly it!"

The Tweetle disappeared from the window. The rocket lifted and hovered for a moment,

then tipped over on its side with a horrible, grunching clang.

Ricky sprang the escape hatch. Inside, the Tweetle was curled up, fast asleep.

Sue called from an upstairs window. "Ricky, come quick! They're going crazy!"

In the bathroom, a middle-sized
Tweetle was squirting toothpaste
and puffs of shaving foam into the
air and catching them in its mouth.

Another was lapping water out of
the toilet bowl. It licked its lips,
hiccupped and smiled.

The other two Tweetles were
dancing up and down in front of
a mirror, smearing Mum's lipstick
on their faces and singing in strange,
bird-like tones.

A voice boomed from downstairs. "What's going on?" Dad had come home and Mr Tweetle was with him!

Dad stormed upstairs. "Someone has given these Tweetles sucrose!"

"Not us!" Ricky protested. "All they've had is shortbread astronauts."

"And what's in these shortbread astronauts?" Dad asked.

"Um… Flour?"

"Yes…"said Dad.

"Um… Butter?"

"Yes…"said Dad.

"Um… Sugar?"
Dad exploded. "Sugar!
Sugar is sucrose!"

Mum came to the rescue. "We used
Granny Earth's recipe book. It says to
use sugar. Ricky wasn't to know that
sugar and sucrose are the same thing!"

"Never mind," said Mrs Tweetle. "They'll be all right, but they're going to have terrible headaches tomorrow! The only biscuits we have in our house are Lord Vorg crunchy bars. At least you know what's in them!"

By now, all the little Tweetles were fast asleep and floating a metre off the ground. Mr Tweetle had to tie some string round their legs and walk them home like a bunch of balloons.

LIZARDS FROM THE PLANET LANDY

HAPPY WAGGY TAIL

Laughing Landy Lizards make everyone laugh. There is a one hour teevee show of just the Lizards laughing at the camera.

It is impossible not to laugh with them.

Landy Lizards laugh when they are sad or depressed.

THE LANDY LIZARD SHOW

DON'T MAKE ME LAUGH!

However, the Lizards make a lot of money from their teevee show, which cheers them up a bit.

Dad helped Ricky put his rocket back on its landing pads. "Make sure you don't give the Tweetles anything with sugar in it the next time you see them!"

Mum came out into the yard. "Is everything OK with Mr Tweetle now?"

"Yes, thank goodness. In fact, he's invited us over for tea on Sunday."

"Hurray!" Ricky whooped. "The only biscuits they have in their house are Lord Vorg crunchy bars!"

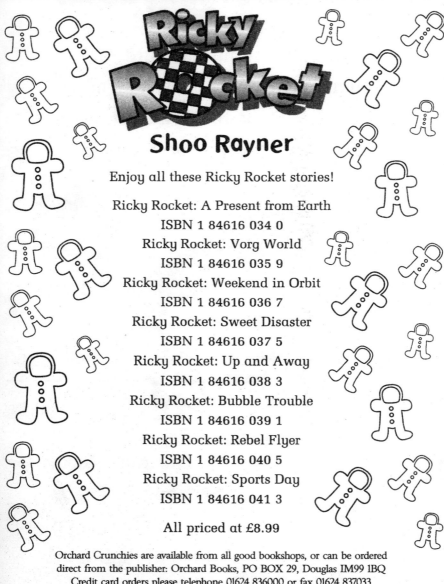

Shoo Rayner

Enjoy all these Ricky Rocket stories!

All priced at £8.99

Orchard Crunchies are available from all good bookshops, or can be ordered
direct from the publisher: Orchard Books, PO BOX 29, Douglas IM99 1BQ
Credit card orders please telephone 01624 836000 or fax 01624 837033
or visit our internet site: www.wattspub.co.uk or e-mail: bookshop@enterprise.net for details.

To order please quote title, author and ISBN and your full name and address.
Cheques and postal orders should be made payable to 'Bookpost plc.'
Postage and packing is FREE within the UK
(overseas customers should add £1.00 per book).

Prices and availability are subject to change.